DO I HAVE TO SAY HELLO?

Also by Delia Ephron

FUNNY SAUCE
SANTA AND ALEX

(with drawings by Edward Koren)
TEENAGE ROMANCE
HOW TO EAT LIKE A CHILD

DO I HAVE TO SAY HELLO?

Aunt Delia's Manners Quiz for Kids and Their Grownups

DELIA EPHRON
With drawings by EDWARD KOREN

Viking

VIKING
Published by the Penguin Group
Viking Penguin, a division of Penguin Books USA Inc.,
40 West 23rd Street, New York, New York 10010, U.S.A.
Penguin Books Ltd, 27 Wrights Lane,
London W8 5TZ, England
Penguin Books Australia Ltd, Ringwood,
Victoria, Australia
Penguin Books Canada Ltd, 2801 John Street,
Markham, Ontario, Canada L3R 1B4
Penguin Books (N.Z.) Ltd, 182–190 Wairau Road,
Auckland 10, New Zealand

Penguin Books Ltd, Registered Offices:
Harmondsworth, Middlesex, England

First published in 1989 by Viking Penguin,
a division of Penguin Books USA Inc.

1   3   5   7   9   10   8   6   4   2

LIBRARY OF CONGRESS CATALOGING IN PUBLICATION DATA
Ephron, Delia.
Do I Have to Say Hello?: Aunt Delia's manners quiz
for kids and their grownups
Delia Ephron: with drawings by Edward Koren.
        p.   cm.
ISBN 0-670-82855-6
1. Etiquette — Humor.   I. Title.
PN6231.E8E64   1989
818'.5401 — dc20   88-40652

Printed in the United States of America

Set in Frutiger Light 45
Designed by Lorraine Bodger

Lucky you.
It's from Aunt Delia.

How do you reply?

"Go jump in the lake."

"I hate tests."

"What does cordially mean?"

"Okay, but I'm bringing forty friends. You'd better have food."

"I don't really want to but my mom wants me to."

"I'd love to, Aunt Delia. Thank you so much for asking me."

If you accepted the invitation, what do you do now?

Turn the page.

Close the book and throw it out the window.

Contents

Contents

DO I HAVE TO SAY HELLO?

TABLE MANNERS

Your aunt is making dinner and she asks you to set the table.
Do you say, "I can't. I'm busy"?
Do you moan and say, "Oh, okay, but I'm so tired"?
Do you say, "Why should I have to set the table? Why doesn't Uncle Jerry? He never does anything"?
Do you say, "Sure, Aunt Delia"?

You put down placemats, plates, forks, knives, spoons, napkins, and glasses. Finally you're finished. What do you say?

"Would you like me to do anything else, Aunt Delia?"

"Okay, I did it, but next time, do it yourself."

Dinner is ready. You sit down. Where do you put your napkin?

Around your neck.

On your head.

In your lap.

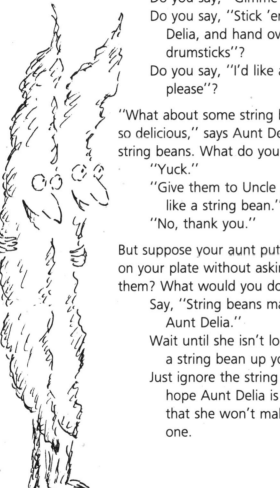

Now your aunt is serving. She asks if you would like some chicken.

> Do you say, "Gimme"?
>
> Do you say, "Stick 'em up, Aunt Delia, and hand over your drumsticks"?
>
> Do you say, "I'd like a drumstick please"?

"What about some string beans? They're so delicious," says Aunt Delia. You hate string beans. What do you say?

> "Yuck."
>
> "Give them to Uncle Jerry. He looks like a string bean."
>
> "No, thank you."

But suppose your aunt puts string beans on your plate without asking if you want them? What would you do then?

> Say, "String beans make me barf, Aunt Delia."
>
> Wait until she isn't looking and put a string bean up your nose.
>
> Just ignore the string beans and hope Aunt Delia is nice enough that she won't make you just eat one.

Do any of these drawings show the proper way to sit while you eat?

Which of these is it okay to do while you eat dinner with your aunt and uncle?

> Beat your chest and yell, "Me, Tarzan."
> Peel your scab.
> Listen to your Walkman.
> Read.
> Talk.
> Snore.

Which of these are not appropriate subjects for dinner-table conversation?

> What Aunt Delia and Uncle Jerry did at work today.
> Tushies.
> The dead rat in Uncle Jerry and Aunt Delia's garage.
> Throw-up.
> Mucus.
> What you want to be when you grow up.
> That Aunt Delia looks about a hundred years old.
> Whether you can say without making a mistake, "One smart fellow, he felt smart. Two smart fellows, they felt smart. Three smart fellows, they all felt smart."

You want another helping of corn.

> Do you say, "Please pass the corn, Uncle Jerry"?
> Do you say, "Yo, corn"?
> Do you bang the table with your knife until Aunt Delia and Uncle Jerry ask what you want?

When your uncle passes the corn, you notice that there is just a little bit left and nobody else has had seconds yet. You are the first. What do you do?

> Ask, ''Does anyone else want seconds?'' so that you can leave a little for other people at the table.
> Say, ''Aunt Delia, you didn't make enough.''
> Take it all.

Suppose you took it all and then as soon as you put a big forkful of corn in your mouth, Aunt Delia asked what happened at school today?

> Do you wait until you're finished chewing and then tell her?
> Do you answer, spraying corn across the table?
> Do you open your mouth and point at what's inside so your aunt figures out you can't talk?

Uncle Jerry burps by accident.

Do you fall off your chair laughing?

Do you keep eating, pretending you don't think it's funny because you don't want to embarrass Uncle Jerry?

You burp on purpose.

Do you fall off your chair laughing?

Do you say, "Excuse me"?

Uh-oh, you have to sneeze.

Do you cover your mouth and nose with your napkin and then do it?

Do you aim straight at the chicken and then do it?

Do you say, "Surprise, Uncle Jerry," and do it in his face?

Uh-oh, Uncle Jerry has to sneeze.

Do you duck?

Do you say, "God bless you, Uncle Jerry"?

Do you chant, "Do it again, do it again. I like it, I like it"?

You are finished eating. What do you do with your knife and fork?

Put them in your hair as if they were barrettes.

Stab your leftover meat with them so they poke up like flagpoles.

Place them lying down, side by side on the plate.

What is the proper way to wipe your mouth?
    With your hand.
    With your T-shirt.
    With your napkin.

What is the proper way to inform your aunt and uncle that you are finished and would like to leave the table?
    A burp.
    "May I please be excused?"
    "See ya."

TELEPHONE MANNERS

This is the incorrect way to hold the receiver.

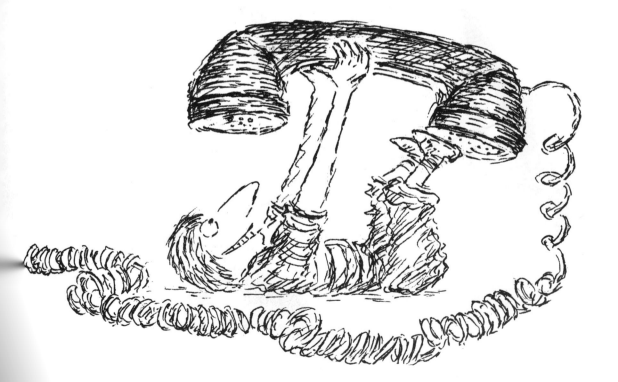

This is the correct way.

In which of these telephone calls are you using good manners?

The phone is ringing.
Pick up the receiver.
Listen.
Say nothing.

The phone is ringing. Answer it.
"Hello."
"Hello. May I please speak to Delia?"
"Huh?"
"Is this Delia's nephew?"
"Uh-huh."
"May I please speak to your aunt?"
Put down the receiver and go back to watching television.

The phone is ringing. Answer it.
"Hello."
"Hello. May I please speak to Delia?"
"I'm sorry. My aunt isn't home right now. May I take a
    message?"
"This is Mrs. Beaman calling."
"Would you please spell that?"
"B-E-A-M-A-N."
"Does my aunt have your phone number?"
"It's 555-9881."
"Thank you, Mrs. Beaman. I'll tell my aunt to call you as soon as
    she gets home. Good-bye."

The phone is ringing. Answer it.
"Who is this?"
"This is Mrs. Beaman. Who is this?"
"None of your business."
"Oh. Well, may I please speak to Delia?"

"Maybe."
"Is she home?"
"Maybe."
"Would you go look?"
"No, I'm too tired."
Hang up.

The phone is ringing. Aunt Delia is home now. Answer the
phone.
"Hello."
"Hello. May I please speak to Delia?"
"It'll cost ya."
"Excuse me?"
"I said, 'If you want my aunt, you'll have to pay.' "
"I'll call back later."
"Suit yourself."

The phone is ringing. Aunt Delia is home. Answer
the phone.
"Hello."
"May I please speak to Delia?"
"Yes. May I tell her who's calling?"
"Mrs. Beaman."
"Just a minute please."
Put the receiver down. "Aunt Delia, it's
    for you. It's Mrs. Beaman."

The phone is ringing. Aunt Delia is
still home. Answer the phone.
"Walnut factory. Head nut speaking."
"May I please speak to Delia?"
"Wrong number."

The Sharing Chart

Select the drawings in which you are
sharing generously with your friend.

CAKE

APPLE

BANANA

GUM

BIRTHDAY PARTY MANNERS

It's your birthday today. You are having a big party and are so excited. Your friend Polly arrives. What's the first thing you say to her?

"What did you bring me?"

"Hi, Polly. I'm so glad you could come."

"Polly want a cracker?"

"Who invited you? There must be some mistake."

Guest Behavior Bonus Question

What's the first thing you say to the birthday girl?

"Happy birthday."

"My mother made me come."

"Where's the food?"

Polly doesn't go to your school so she doesn't know anyone else at the party.

> Do you say, "Polly, these are my friends, Naomi and Max. Naomi and Max, this is Polly"?
>
> Do you say, "Good luck trying to meet kids"?
>
> Do you say, "Naomi and Max, this is poor, pitiful Polly. She doesn't have any friends"?

All the guests are here. It's time for Uncle Jerry to do his magic tricks. Everyone has to sit on the grass and be quiet. Which is the best way to ask your guests to do this?

> Call out, "Okay, everyone. Time for the magic show. Please sit on the grass and be quiet."
>
> Shout, "Sit down and shut up."

Everyone sits down for the show. When you go to take your seat, you discover that there's no room for you in the front row.

> Do you sit in the back row?
>
> Do you say, "You have to sit in back, Naomi," and take her seat?
>
> Do you cry?

Now it gets tricky. Suppose you told Naomi to sit in back and she refused. What would you do then?

> Stamp your foot and shout, "I'M THE BIRTHDAY GIRL. IT'S MY DAY. EVERYONE MUST DO WHAT I SAY."
>
> Pull Naomi's hair.
>
> Say, "Oh, okay," and sit in back.

Uncle Jerry needs a helper for his trick where he puts an egg in a hat and pulls out a fried chicken. He asks for a volunteer.

Do you raise your hand?

Do you say, "Uncle Jerry, may I please speak to you privately?" and explain that if he expects to get a slice of cake, he'd better make *you* the magician's helper?

Do you shout, "The birthday girl gets to choose," and then choose yourself?

Which guests are behaving badly during the magic show?

When the magic show is over, what do you do?
Applaud.
Boo.
Throw things.

Guest Behavior Bonus Question

Uh-oh, you get a telephone call right in the middle of your birthday party. It's John. He wasn't invited and he doesn't know you're having a party.

> Do you say, "I can't talk now, John. May I call you back later?"

> Do you say, "What a dumb time to call—right in the middle of my birthday party"?

> Do you hold the phone receiver in the direction of the party so he can hear all the noise and then say, "So what do you think that was?"

It's time to choose teams for the relay race. Polly doesn't want to play because she's shy.

> Do you ignore her?

> Do you chant, "Polly's a party pooper, Polly's a party pooper"?

> Do you say, "Polly, I'd really like it if you'd play. You can be on my team. I'll show you how"?

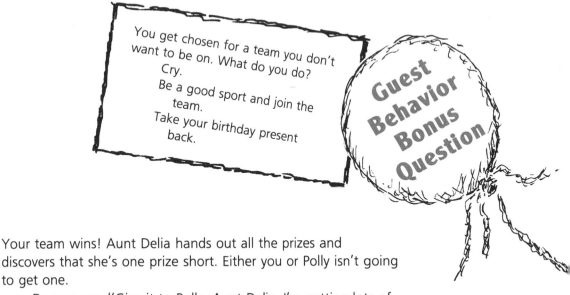

You get chosen for a team you don't want to be on. What do you do?
Cry.
Be a good sport and join the team.
Take your birthday present back.

Guest Behavior Bonus Question

Your team wins! Aunt Delia hands out all the prizes and discovers that she's one prize short. Either you or Polly isn't going to get one.

Do you say, "Give it to Polly, Aunt Delia. I'm getting lots of presents today"?

Do you say, "I want it. It's my birthday"?

Do you burst into tears and cry until Polly feels so bad that she tells Aunt Delia to give the prize to you?

Do you throw the prize in the bushes so no one gets it?

Which of these things is it okay for the birthday girl to say while she cuts the cake?

"Raise your hand if you think I'm pretty."

"Sit down and shut up."

"Who wants a rose on his slice?"

"I'm giving chocolate ice cream to kids I really, really like, and vanilla to those I only sort of like."

Do any of these drawings show the proper thing to do with your cup when you are finished with your Hawaiian Punch?

Everyone is sitting around watching you open presents except
Max, who is busy learning a magic trick from your Uncle Jerry.

   Do you start unwrapping presents even though he's not
      paying attention?

   Do you shout, "Max, watch me"?

   Do you start crying and tell Uncle Jerry he's ruining your
      party by taking all your friends away?

The first present you open is just what you always wanted.

Do you say,"Thank you, Jacob, this is just what I've always wanted"?

Do you throw it down and start opening the next one?

Do you say, "Oh, I love this. How much did it cost?"

Suppose you asked how much it cost and Jacob said, "Fifteen dollars." What would you say then?

"Your money or your mom's?"

"Cheap-O."

"Wow!"

Your aunt asks to speak to you privately and says that it's not good manners to ask the price of presents. "How much it costs doesn't matter," says Aunt Delia. "It's the thought that counts."

Do you say, "Mind your own business, Aunt Delia"?

Do you say to Jacob, "That was a good thought even if it was a cheap one"?

Do you say no more to Jacob about the cost of his present and not ask the cost of any other presents either?

Guest Behavior Bonus Question

When the birthday girl opens your present and thanks you, what do you say?

"It was on sale."

"Don't thank me, thank my mom. She paid for it."

"You're welcome."

Your second present is a book that you have already read.

Do you say, "Thank you, Anna"?

Do you say, "I've already read this"?

Do you say, "Who wants this?" and give it to a kid who raises his hand?

Your next present is a very funny-looking sweater that you would never wear.

Do you say, "Thank you very much, Hilary"?

Do you say, "This is the most beautiful sweater I have ever seen. I will treasure it always"?

Do you say, "This is the ugliest sweater I have ever seen. I will put it in the garbage"?

Do you burst out laughing?

Do you pretend to throw up?

After unwrapping all the presents, the party's over. Polly's mom is the first to arrive. Aunt Delia says, "You remember Polly's mom, don't you, dear?" What do you say?

"Remember her? I have nightmares about her."

"Don't shake my hand, it's sweaty."

"Hello. It's very nice to see you again."

"Who's Polly?"

Polly says, "Thank you for having me."

Do you say, "Thank you for coming"?

Do you say, "Well, everyone makes mistakes"?

Do you say, "You were very fortunate to have been invited to my party. I may consider inviting you again but I'm not sure. Perhaps if you call to remind me around this time next year, you might be lucky enough to be on the guest list. Ta, ta"?

Tricky Question 1

Who has the butter knife?

CAR MANNERS

Uncle Jerry is taking you and your cousin Matt to the movies. "Tell us a story," you say to Uncle Jerry. "Okay," says Uncle Jerry. "I'll tell you a story but you have to find the crazy parts."

"Once upon a time, your Uncle Jerry was taking you and Matt to the movies. You and Matt got into an argument—'I want to sit in front!' 'No, me!' Uncle Jerry suggested that the best way to settle the argument was for you and Matt to hit each other. So after you slugged Matt and he slugged you, and Uncle Jerry congratulated you on being so well-behaved, you both got in the back seat and immediately unfastened your seat belts. Then you rolled down the window and stuck your heads out so you could say hi to drivers going by. 'Good move,' said Uncle Jerry. 'I know Aunt Delia thinks that the safest way to ride is with your head out the window.'

"The traffic suddenly got terrible. Bumper to bumper. To help Uncle Jerry concentrate, you grabbed his glasses. 'Thanks,' said Uncle Jerry. Then you put your hands over his eyes and said, 'Guess who?'

" 'Oh, boy, now I can really see clearly,' said Uncle Jerry.

"As the traffic crept along, you saw the reason for the traffic jam—a big truck stuck in the road. You stood on the seat to get a better view. 'Stand on tiptoe,' said Uncle Jerry. 'That way if I stop short you won't get hurt.'

'' 'I'm starved, Uncle Jerry,' you said. 'Gimme a banana.'

'' 'I love it when you're so polite,' said Uncle Jerry. He took both hands off the wheel so he could get one for you. 'The car will drive itself,' said Uncle Jerry. You unpeeled the banana and dropped the peel on the floor because you didn't want to get the plastic garbage bag dirty. A couple of pieces of banana fell into your lap by accident while you ate. 'What do I do with these?' you asked Uncle Jerry. 'Squash them into the seat,' said Uncle Jerry. 'That's the most considerate thing to do because then Aunt Delia will sit on them and get them on her pants. Aunt Delia loves banana stains.'

'' 'I want juice now. Get it for me or else,' you said to Uncle Jerry.

'' 'What a sweet way to ask,' said Uncle Jerry, handing you a small can of apple juice.

''You drank it quickly and threw the can out the window. 'Good for you,' said Uncle Jerry. 'Cans and flowers look so pretty together and you don't want to get the plastic garbage bag dirty.'

''Then you discovered that Matt's foot was on your side of the seat. 'Kick him,' said Uncle Jerry. 'If someone is on your side, the best thing to do is to give him a big fat kick.' So you kicked Matt and Uncle Jerry said, 'Okay, Matt, kick him back.' Matt did.

" 'Wasn't that a smart way to solve the problem?' asked Uncle Jerry.

" 'Yes, we feel so grown up,' said you and Matt together.

" 'Aunt Delia will be so proud of you for kicking,' said Uncle Jerry.

" 'Oh, look, we're here,' said Matt.

"Uncle Jerry parked the car, you fastened your seat belt, and got out. The end."

"I hope you liked that story," says Uncle Jerry. Then he gives you a bonus question.

Put these three sentences in the order in which they should take place.
a) Throw up.
b) Get out of the car.
c) Ask Uncle Jerry to pull over.

Car Bonus Question

BEACH MANNERS

Your Aunt Delia unpacks the car:
five towels, a blanket, a cooler, one pail,
a shovel, her tote bag, and a beach umbrella.
She asks you to help carry something.
Do you say, "Sure, Aunt Delia"?
Do you say, "I'm too weak"?
Do you stop a man going by and say, "Excuse me but my
aunt thinks you look awfully cute in a bathing suit.
Would you help her carry stuff?"

The beach is very crowded. You'll have enough room to put
down your towels if you can get one family to move a little bit to
the left. What would be the polite way to accomplish this?
Ask them, "Would you mind moving over a little to the
left?"
Kick sand on them from the right.
Say, "Move it. What are you trying to do—hog the place?"

Which of these things should sand be used for?
    Building sand castles.
    Burying Aunt Delia.
    Sprinkling on sandwiches.
    Throwing.

Which of these things is it okay to say in a loud voice at the beach?
    "Oh, it's so beautiful here."
    "The sand in my suit is making my tushy itch."
    "Why is that man so fat?"
    "Boy, did that bathroom smell."
    "Aunt Delia, that woman isn't wearing a top."
    "Sharks, sharks!"

You see a kid building a sand castle. You want to help.

Do you tell him your name and ask, "May I please help?"

Do you knock his sand castle over and then say, "Awww, look what happened to your sand castle. You probably need help building another"?

Do you say, "What ugly turrets. I'll fix them"?

Do you say, "I'm a much better sand-castle builder than you are. Do you want to see how much better I can make this?"

There is a girl playing in the water. What is a good thing to say if you want to make friends with her?

"Hi. Do you want to play?"

"My aunt and uncle are very rich and I'm going to inherit all their money."

"You probably want to be my friend because I've met Madonna."

"You probably don't want to be my friend, but just in case you do, here's my name."

Beach Towel Bonus Questions

Yes or No Answers Only

It is a good idea to wave your beach towel in the air so sand flies into the food.

It is a good idea to wave your beach towel in the air so sand flies into Aunt Delia's face.

People love it when you snap a wet towel at them.

Aunt Delia will love it if you turn all your sand crabs loose on her towel.

Beach towels make good rafts.

When you go home, you should leave your beach towel on the sand to be used by the next person who comes to the beach.

Aunt Delia gasps, "Oh my goodness, I forgot to put sun block on
you. Come here."
    Do you say, "No"?
    Do you let Aunt Delia cover you with lotion?
    Do you say, "Too late," and jump in the water?

After lunch, what do you do with the garbage?
    See if it floats.
    Throw it in the trash can.
    Sit on it.

Now it's time to go home. Aunt Delia asks you to help carry
things to the car.
    Do you say, "Sure"?
    Do you say, "I'm too weak"?
    Do you shout, "Bathing beauty contest—Men Only! Winner
      gets to help my aunt"?

The Eating Chart

Which of these foods
are you eating properly?

PEAS

MASHED POTATOES

CHEERIOS

NACHOS

JELLO

SPAGHETTI

OATMEAL
RAISIN
COOKIE

ICE CREAM

VISITING MANNERS

Your uncle takes you to meet his friends, Steven and Sylvia Madrid. Uncle Jerry says, "Steven, Sylvia, I'd like you to meet my nephew whom I've told you so much about."

Do you say, "What smells?"

Do you say, "Hello, Mrs. Madrid," and shake her hand and then do the same with Mr. Madrid?

Do you look at your shoes?

Do you mumble "Hi" and pick your nose?

Do you cling to your uncle and say, "I want to go home"?

Mrs. Madrid asks, "Are you hungry? Would you like something to eat?"

    Do you say, "Yes, please"?

    Do you pull up your shirt, point to your stomach, and say, "Belly wants cookie"?

    Do you say, "You bet your fat bottom"?

"Oreos, Mallomars, or homemade chocolate chip—which kind would you like?" asks Mrs. Madrid.

    Do you say, "Are there nuts in the chocolate chip or are the only nuts in this house you and Mr. Madrid?"

    Do you say, "I'd like chocolate chip, please"?

    Do you say, "I'll grunt once for Oreos, twice for Mallomars, and three times for chocolate chip"?

After you eat a cookie, you are thirsty. What do you do?

    Say, "Mrs. Madrid, may I please have something to drink?"

    Say to your uncle, "Boy, I sure am thirsty," and hope Mrs. Madrid gets the message.

    Walk into the kitchen, take a 7 Up out of the refrigerator, pop the top, and start drinking.

    Say, "Mrs. Madrid, there are two kinds of people in this world. People who offer their guests something to drink and people who let their guests die of thirst. Which kind are you?"

While you all sit around the table, what would be a good way to start a conversation with Mr. Madrid?

"Do you wear false teeth?"

"What's your favorite baseball team?"

"May I please see your pajamas?"

"Uncle Jerry's underpants are purple."

Let's say you asked Mr. Madrid about his favorite baseball team, and he said,"I don't like any of them." What would be a good way to change the subject?

"Have you ever considered going on a diet?"

"Who are you voting for in the next election?"

"Your nose is peeling."

Conversation Bonus Question

After discussing the election with Mr. Madrid, what would be a good way to start a conversation with Mrs. Madrid?

"Tell me, Mrs. Madrid, do you get much ear wax?"

"Have you ever eaten a fly?"

"Seen any good movies lately?"

"How much did your house cost?"

Now you're bored. Uncle Jerry and the Madrids are discussing income-tax deductions. What should you do?

Climb to the top of the china cabinet.

Throw a tantrum on the rug.

Torture Mrs. Madrid's beloved dog Daisy.

Read.

Your Uncle Jerry finally says it's time to leave. Aunt Delia will be wondering what happened to you.

Do you say, "Good-bye. It was very nice to meet you"?

Do you shout, "Hurray, I'm free"?

Do you suck your thumb and just stand there?

Do you say, "Good-bye, Mr. and Mrs. Madrid. You have a very weird name and I hope I never see you again"?

ASKING MANNERS

Your friend Molly asks you
to sleep over. You have to get
permission from Aunt Delia.
In which of these conversations
are you asking politely?

"Aunt Delia, may I please sleep at Molly's?"
"Yes, dear."
"Thank you."

"Aunt Delia, may I please sleep at Molly's?"
"It's a school night."
"If I promise to do all my homework before I go and go to
    sleep at nine o'clock, may I do it just this once?"
"All right, if you promise."

"I'm sleeping at Molly's, Aunt Delia, and I told her you'd
    take me."
"What? It's out of the question. First of all, you didn't ask
    permission. Second, it's a school night."
"Molly said you should get me there by six o'clock."
"I said you're not going."
"Here are the car keys, Aunt Delia. Get in and start
    driving."

"Aunt Delia, I promised Molly I'd sleep over."

"I'm sorry, you can't—it's a school night."

"But I promised."

"You should have asked me first."

"But you weren't here."

"Then you should have told Molly that you couldn't give her an answer until I got home."

"But Molly's expecting me, her mom's expecting me, her dad's expecting me, they made a special chocolate cake in honor of my arrival. I make them happy. I cheer them up. You'll ruin their whole day if you don't let me go. Is that what you want?"

"I have to sleep over at Molly's tonight because it's our homework assignment."

"Your homework assignment?"

"Yes, and if I don't do it, I'll fail."

"May I please sleep at Molly's?"

"No."

"Okay."

"Please, beautiful aunt, gorgeous aunt, sweetest aunt, aunt whom I love more than anything else in the world, may I sleep at Molly's?"

"No. It's a school night."

"I hate you."

"Aunt Delia, say, 'Y.' "
"Y."
"Now say, 'E.' "
"E."
"Now say, 'S.' "
"S."
"Thanks, Aunt Delia. Molly, Aunt Delia says I can sleep
over."

BASEBALL MANNERS

Your team, the Panthers, is playing the
Tigers. It's your turn to bat. You step
into the batter's box. What do you do?
Take a few practice swings.
Kiss the catcher.
Look down to see if your fly is zipped.

Uncle Jerry and Aunt Delia are sitting in the stands watching you
play. What does Uncle Jerry shout when you are at bat?
"Come on, baby, hit it out of the park."
"You forgot to make your bed and you can't play until
you do."
"Keep your eye off the ball."

You hit the ball and run. What do you do with the bat?
Drop it.
Carry it to first and hit the first baseman
over the head with it.
Toss it to the crowd.

You steal second, the catcher
makes the throw, and the
umpire calls it—you're out! You
think you're safe. What do you do?
Leave the field quietly.
Leave the field and take second base
with you.
Sit down on second base and refuse
to get up.
Tell the umpire he's a stupid,
cross-eyed dope who couldn't
see the Grand Canyon if he fell into
it, and keep screaming at him until
the coach carries you off the field.

Uncle Jerry, watching from the stands, thinks you're safe, too.
What does Uncle Jerry do?
Nothing.
Punches the umpire.
Starts crying and has to be comforted by Aunt Delia.
Goes to the coach and insists that he stop the game.
Nobody treats his nephew like that. Nobody!

Now your team is in the field. You want to play shortstop but the coach says, "Sorry, today you're playing left field." What do you say?

"Okay, Coach, whatever you say."

"My mitt doesn't work in left field, it only works at shortstop."

"My Uncle Jerry says that if you don't let me play shortstop, he'll have you fired."

A batter hits a long fly your way. You run for it, put your mitt up to catch it, and boom!—it lands on the ground behind you. What do you do?

Pick up the ball and throw to second.

Shout, "It's not fair. The sun was in my eyes."

Run off the field crying.

What does Uncle Jerry say when you miss the ball?
  "Good try."
  "If you'd made your bed that wouldn't have happened."
  "I was going to take you to McDonald's but now that
    you've messed up, I won't."

Your team wins. What do you do?
  Shout, "Two, four, six, eight, who do
    we appreciate? The Tigers, the
    Tigers, yeah."
  Shout, "The Tigers stink and we
    proved it."

Tricky Question 2

How do you cut your meat?
>With scissors.
>With a knife.
>With a saw.

RESTAURANT MANNERS

Aunt Delia and Uncle Jerry are taking you to Caffe Italiano, a very fancy restaurant. You are all dressed up. When you walk in, the maître d' asks, "Do you have a reservation?" "Yes," says Uncle Jerry. "Kass, for three." The maître d' shows you to your table. What do you do?

Refuse to sit down unless you can sit next to Aunt Delia.

Sit down and put your napkin in your lap.

Ask the maître d' if the plants are real.

You read the menu and discover that you don't know what half the things are, and besides, the restaurant doesn't have hamburgers. Oh, no! What do you say?

"There's nothing here I want to eat."

"They don't have hamburgers so I guess I'll have squid."

"Aunt Delia, I'm not sure what I want. Could you please help me pick?"

Aunt Delia suggests that you would either like the ravioli in tomato sauce with mushrooms, or the tortellini Alfredo. The waiter comes to take your order. "What would you like?" he asks.

Do you say, "Guess"?

Do you say, "I didn't ask you what you're having for dinner. I don't see why you should ask me"?

Do you say, "I'd like ravioli in tomato sauce, but no mushrooms and no cheese on top, please, and a Coke. Thank you"?

"You've already had one Coke today," says Aunt Delia. "I think you should order milk or juice." What do you say?

"I hate you."

"Mom always lets me have two Cokes."

"Okay, Aunt Delia."

Now it gets tricky. Suppose you answered, "Mom always lets me have two Cokes," but you secretly know that she doesn't. And your Aunt Delia, surprised, says, "Does your mom really let you have two Cokes?"

Do you say, "Yes"?

Do you say, "Aunt Delia, would I lie to you? I love you so much. You are my best aunt," and give her a gigantic kiss?

Do you say, "Well, I'm not sure. I guess I'll just have milk, please"?

"Your dinner comes with soup or salad," says the waiter. "What kind of soup?" asks Aunt Delia. "Minestrone," says the waiter. What do you say?

"I'll have minestrone, please."

"I'll have the soup, because the last time I had salad, I got a stomachache."

While you are waiting for your food, what do you do?

Eat the insides of sixteen pieces of bread and announce that you're full.

Play tic-tac-toe with Uncle Jerry.

Put the ashtray on your head.

Complain.

Stand on the seat and check out the people at the table next to yours.

The waiter brings the soup. You are about to eat it when you notice that there's a fly in it.

Do you swat it?

Do you eat it?

Do you say, "Excuse me," to the waiter, "but a fly is
swimming in my soup"?

Now you have to go to the bathroom.

> Do you stand on your chair and shout, "I have to pee"?
>
> Do you say quietly to your aunt and uncle, "Excuse me, I have to go to the bathroom"?

But you can't find the bathroom. You have to ask a waiter.

> Do you say,"Excuse me, would you please tell me where the rest room is?"
>
> Do you say, "Hurry, quick. Where's the toilet? I gotta go"?

When the waiter brings your ravioli, he also puts down a little side dish of zucchini. What do you say?

> "Yikes! I didn't order that."
>
> "Euu, gross."
>
> "Thank you."

Good grief. You take a big bite of ravioli and discover that there's a mushroom in the tomato sauce and you specifically asked for no mushrooms. What do you do?

Wave frantically at the waiter and when he comes over, open your mouth and show him what's inside.

Put your napkin to your mouth and, without attracting attention, get the mushroom out of your mouth and into your napkin.

Spit the mushroom into your milk.

It's time for dessert. "We have spumoni, tortoni, cannoli, tartufo, and chocolate cake," says the waiter. You pick chocolate cake. "Can I have a bite?" asks Uncle Jerry.

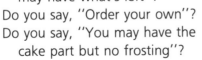

Do you say, "Sure," and pass him your plate?

Do you say, "When I'm done, you may have what's left"?

Do you say, "Order your own"?

Do you say, "You may have the cake part but no frosting"?

You are leaving the restaurant with your aunt and uncle. Your private opinion of the food was that the ravioli tasted like rubber but that the chocolate cake was delicious. Which of these things would it be right to say?

"Thank you for taking me, Uncle Jerry."

"Those ravioli tasted like rubber."

"Get me out of here fast."

"I really loved the chocolate cake."

"My dad takes me to much nicer places that cost a lot more money."

The Noise Chart

Which noises are acceptable
at the dinner table?

THANK YOU MANNERS

Mr. and Mrs. Madrid sent you a red turtleneck for Christmas.
Aunt Delia says that you have to write them a thank-you note.
Which of these would be the most polite to send?

Dear Mr. and Mrs. Madrid,
     Thank you for the sweater.
     P.S. Aunt Delia made me write this.

Dear Mr. and Mrs. Madrid,
     I had the greatest Christmas. I got Western Barbie, a disguise kit, slippers, a laser helmet, walkie-talkies, sponges that turn into dinosaurs, and an ant farm, so I don't mind at all that you gave me that gross, ugly, disgusting sweater.

Dear Mr. and Mrs. Madrid,
     Thank you very much for the beautiful red sweater. It fits perfectly. I can't wait to wear it to school. I hope you had a very happy Christmas.

Dear Mr. and Mrs. Madrid,
     Thank you for the ketchup-colored sweater. When I wear it, I look like a hamburger.

Yo, Madrids,
     What's happening? How's life at your weird old house? Do you still have Daisy the dog or did you make her into sausages, ha, ha, ha. By the way, thanks.

Dear Mr. and Mrs. Madrid,
     Thanks for whatever you gave me. I opened my presents so fast that all the cards got mixed up. But who cares anyway. The whole point of Christmas is to get a lot and I sure did.

SCHOOL MANNERS

MULTIPLE CHOICE TEST

To describe the proper way to behave in class, complete the following sentences correctly.

As usual, you arrive in class . . .
- a) wearing pajamas.
- b) with a stocking on your head.
- c) on time.

You are chewing three pieces of bubble gum. Before taking your seat, you . . .
- a) throw the gum in the waste basket.
- b) stick it under your desk.
- c) offer to entertain the class by blowing a bubble while dancing the hula.

Your teacher, Mrs. Fox, asks you to pass your homework to the front of the class and you . . .

    a) refuse.
    b) take it out of your notebook and pass it.
    c) make it into a paper airplane and send it airmail.

You want to know if there will be a spelling test today. To get Mrs. Fox's attention, you . . .

    a) throw a spitball.
    b) raise your hand.
    c) burp.

Mrs. Fox calls on you, you ask her about the test, and she says, "Yes, we're going to have a test later but first we are going to study great explorers. Open your book to page 100." What page? You didn't hear. Do you . . .

    a) shout, "What page? I didn't hear"?
    b) raise your hand and wait to be called on?
    c) ask a kid sitting next to you?

Mrs. Fox asks if anyone in the class knows which explorer named the Pacific Ocean. You know the answer so you . . .

    a) keep it a secret.
    b) shout, "Balboa."
    c) shout, "I'll give you a hint—he doesn't go to this school."
    d) raise your hand and wait to be called on.

Mrs. Fox calls on Zachary, who doesn't know the answer so he guesses. "Columbus," he says. Columbus! He didn't even see the Pacific! While Mrs. Fox explains that to Zachary you . . .

    a) whisper "dummy" loud enough for Zachary to hear.

    b) keep quiet but raise your hand with the right answer.

    c) wave your hand in Mrs. Fox's face, chanting, "I know it, I know it, me, me, me."

While Mrs. Fox mentions other explorers like Admiral Byrd, you remember that you wanted your friend Jessica to feel your muscles so you . . .

    a) decide to wait until recess to show her.

    b) send her a note, "Meet me at the drinking fountain if you want to feel my muscles."

    c) assume a muscle-man pose with arms bent and hope she notices.

Complete these sentences correctly and you get an *A*.

The best place to doodle is . . .

    a) on your hand.

    b) on a piece of notebook paper.

    c) on the desk.

When the principal visits your class, you should . . .
    a) shout, "Hi, Princy."
    b) keep doing your work quietly.
    c) make smacking noises with your mouth.

Mrs. Fox puts three math problems on the board and asks you to solve them. The first one is very hard so you . . .
    a) start crying.
    b) try to do your best.
    c) look over your friend's shoulder and copy down his
       answer.

You finish early. After double-checking your work, you . . .
    a) draw a picture of Mrs. Fox looking like a gorilla.
    b) sit quietly until Mrs. Fox picks up the papers.
    c) chant, "Done, done, done, done, done."
    d) use your pencils for drumsticks and Zachary's head for a
       drum.
    e) talk to a friend.

The bell rings. It's time to go to recess. Do you . . .
    a) wait until Mrs. Fox dismisses you?
    b) yell, "So long, Foxy," and race out?
    c) refuse to go to recess because you love class so much?

Answer this question correctly and you get an *A* + .

A good present for the teacher is . . .
    a) an apple.
    b) a dead mouse.

The Friendship Test

Answer True or False to the following questions.

If a kid in your class is fat, it's okay to call him Fatso.

If a kid in your class is skinny, it's okay to call her Noodle.

If a kid in your class has a turned-up nose, it's okay to call her Piggy.

If a kid in your class has curly hair, it's okay to call her Frizzball.

If a kid in your class is short, it's okay to call him Shrimp.

If a kid in your class wears glasses, it's okay to call him Four Eyes.

If a kid in your class has a fat behind, it's okay to call him Big Tush.

The Keeping Secrets Test

Select the right answers.

On the way to recess your friend Katie whispers that she has to speak to you privately. "Promise you won't tell?" she asks.
"Yes," you say.
"Are you sure? It's a secret."
"Yes," you say.
"I think Jason is cute," says Katie. Now what do you do?

  a) Say nothing to anyone.
  b) Whisper to your friend Eva, "Katie likes Jason but don't tell, it's a secret."
  c) Tell Jason, "Guess who likes you? Katie."
  d) Climb to the top of the jungle gym and shout, "Attention everyone, Katie wants to marry Jason."

Now the test gets harder. Let's say that you whispered to Jason, "Guess who likes you? Katie. Do you like her?" And he said, "No way! But don't tell, it's a secret. I don't want to hurt her feelings." What would you do then?

  a) Say nothing to anyone.
  b) Send Katie a note that says, "Drop dead," and sign it, "Jason."
  c) Take Katie aside and say that when someone in the class, told Jason that she likes him, he said he was running away to Alaska.

Let's imagine now that it all happened differently. When you told Jason, "Guess who likes you? Katie," he smiled.
"Don't tell, but I like her, too," said Jason. Then what would you do?

  a) Say nothing to anyone.
  b) Tell your friend Eva, "Remember I told you that Katie likes Jason? Well, he likes her but don't tell, it's a secret."
  c) Send out invitations. "You are cordially invited to the wedding of Katie and Jason to be held next recess in front of the jungle gym. Dress casual."

INTERRUPTING MANNERS

You want to tell Aunt Delia
something but she's on the phone
with Mrs. Beaman. What do you do?
  Start talking.
  Wait until she hangs up.
  Cut the phone wires.

Aunt Delia is still on the phone with Mrs. Beaman and you can't wait any longer—what you have to say is very important. What do you do?

Pick up the other extension and scream.

Pick up the other extension and say, "This is the emergency operator with a message for Aunt Delia—get off the phone and pay attention to *me*."

Say, "Excuse me, Aunt Delia, can I talk to you for a minute, it's important?"

Cut the phone wires.

Interrupting Bonus Question

What is important enough to justify interrupting Aunt Delia's telephone conversation?
"Can I watch TV?"
"When's Uncle Jerry coming home?"
"Is it two o'clock yet?"
"I'm hungry."
"Fire!"

Uncle Jerry is in the bathroom and you have to ask him a question. What do you do?

Barge in and surprise him.

Yell, "Are you ever coming out?"

Knock and say, "Excuse me, Uncle Jerry, can I talk to you when you're done?"

Aunt Delia and Uncle Jerry are drinking their morning coffee and
discussing Beirut. You want to tell Uncle Jerry that it's so funny—
Big Bird just sat on the letter *M*. What do you do?

    Say, "Big Bird just sat on the letter *M*."

    Say, "Excuse me, Uncle Jerry, may I please tell you
       something?"

    Say, "I'm so interesting and I know such interesting things.
       Want to hear one?"

Suppose when you said, "May I please tell you something?"
Uncle Jerry said, "Aunt Delia and I are talking. Not now." What
would you do then?

    Say, "Yes, now."

    Wait patiently.

    Start chanting, "Dadadadadadadada," really loudly until
       they can't hear themselves talk and have to listen to you.

As Aunt Delia and Uncle Jerry keep chatting and you wait
patiently, you notice that the heat from the toaster has set the
paper towels on fire. What do you do?

    Wait until they're finished talking.

    Say, "I'm so interesting and I know such interesting things.
       Want to hear one?"

    Shout, "Kitchen, toaster, fire, help!"

MOVIE MANNERS

You are so excited because you are dying to see this movie. Your aunt gives you the money to buy the tickets. There is a very long line.

Do you get at the back of the line and wait your turn?

Do you butt in front of the line?

Do you lean against the wall and moan, "I don't want to stand in line. I'm too tired. Would you carry me, Aunt Delia?"

What do you say to the ticket seller?

"Hi, gorgeous. I'll take two."

"May I please have two tickets—one adult, one child?"

"Hello, my name is Dorothy and I live with Ozma of Oz in the Emerald City. I'll take two free tickets—one for me and one for my Aunt Em."

At the refreshment counter, Aunt Delia gives you some more money and says that you have a choice. Either you can have popcorn and a soda, or you can have a candy bar. What do you say?

"Okay, Aunt Delia."

"I want candy *and* a soda. Maia's mom lets her!"

When you order, what do you say to the girl working behind the counter?

"Kiss me, I'm Irish."

"Bonjour, babycakes. Hand over one package of Milk Duds, a Snickers bar, Hershey with almonds, Gummy Bears, three Sprites, a large popcorn, and send the bill to my aunt."

"May I please have a small popcorn with butter and a Sprite?"

Candy Counter Bonus Question with Ratings

"Would you like anything else?" asks the girl. What do you say now?

G: "No, thank you. That will be all."

PG: "Yes. A big smooch."

PG-13: "Put your hands up and get inside the popcorn machine."

R: "I want *you* covered with butter flavor."

As soon as you sit down in the theater, two kids want to come down your row and sit on the other side of you.

Do you stand up and let them walk by?

Do you put your legs up so they can't get past and say, "Toll bridge, twenty-five cents"?

Do you say, "Sorry, folks. These seats are saved"?

The lights are dimming. The movie's about to begin.

Do you stop talking?

Do you keep talking?

Do you shout, "Quiet everyone. Movie time"?

Uh-oh, you're confused. You can't figure out why that lady in the movie is hiding under her bed and whether that guy is good or bad.

Do you shout, "I'm so mixed up"?

Do you whisper to your aunt, "Why is she under the bed and is he a good guy?"

You just realized who that robber in the movie reminds you of—Mr. Madrid.

Do you tell your aunt right now?

Do you wait until the movie's over?

Do you shout, "Hey, he looks like a friend of mine"?

Let's say that you told your aunt right away and the man sitting behind you said, "Quiet please."

Do you say, "I'm sorry," and stop talking?

Do you say, "Make me"?

Now you have to go to the bathroom but there are several people sitting in your row that you have to go past to get to the aisle. What do you do?

Invite them to come to the bathroom, too.

Climb over them.

Say quietly, "Excuse me," and go past them quickly.

Popcorn Bonus Question with Ratings

You don't want any more popcorn but there is still some left. What are you going to do with it?

G: Put the box on the floor and, when the movie's over, carry it out and put it in the trash can.

PG: Pour it over the head of the kid sitting in front of you.

R: Put it down Aunt Delia's shirt.

The movie's over. When you get home, your aunt reminds you that you forgot to thank her for taking you. What do you say?

"I did, you didn't hear me."

"Thank you, Aunt Delia."

"I don't say thank you. That's just me."

Tricky Question 3

Which of these is the salad fork?

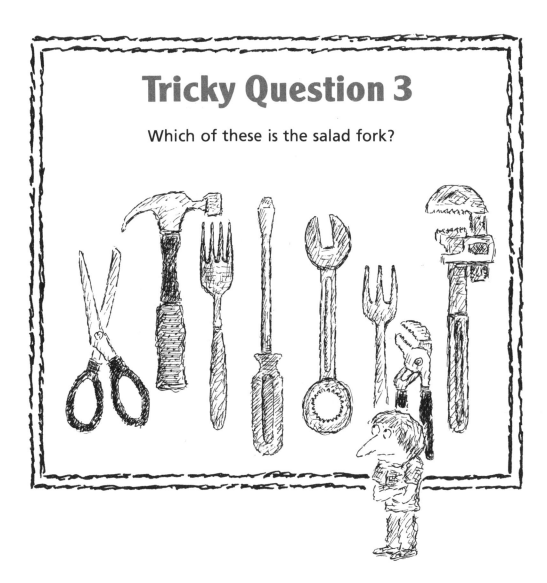

PLAYGROUND MANNERS

Which is the proper way to use the drinking fountain?

Complete the following sentences correctly.

Aunt Delia takes you and your cousin Matt to the playground. All your friends are there. Your aunt sits down on the bench while you and your friend Katie decide to play hopscotch. As soon as you chalk the squares, Sarah comes over. When she asks, "Can I play, too?" you . . .

    a) say, "Sure."

    b) pretend you didn't hear her.

    c) say, "Get lost. The game is private."

Sarah joins in. She throws her marker and then, while hopping from square two to square three, she trips and falls. Oh, dear. Immediately you . . .

    a) help her up.

    b) say, "What a klutz" and start laughing.

    c) shout, "Hey, everyone, look at Sarah."

Sarah starts crying, which makes you feel so bad that you . . .

    a) say, "Shut up, only babies cry."

    b) shout, "Hey, everyone, now she's crying."

    c) put your arm around her while Katie gets your Aunt Delia.

After Aunt Delia washes off Sarah's knee, she buys everyone a
Good Humor bar. You and Katie ask for vanilla inside with
chocolate outside. Sarah orders chocolate inside but you . . .
    a) tell her she has to have vanilla because you say so
       because it's your aunt that's paying.
    b) give her a bite of yours when she gives you one of hers.

You finish your ice cream. To keep the playground clean, you . . .
    a) throw the stick in the garbage can.
    b) ask Aunt Delia to vacuum.
    c) bury the stick in the sandbox.

You continue your game of hopscotch. Now Todd comes over.
"Can I play, too?" he asks. You are about to say, "Yes," when
Sarah whispers in your ear, "Not Todd, he's creepy." So instead
you . . .
    a) say, "Sorry, Todd. No creeps allowed."
    b) tell Sarah that you like Todd and you think that if she
      plays with him, she will, too.
    c) make fun of Todd's flat head so Sarah will like you more.

As soon as you finish playing hopscotch, you get into an
argument about who's stayed up latest. You insist that you've
stayed up until practically four in the morning. Sarah doesn't
believe you. To settle the argument, you . . .
    a) spit at her.
    b) bite her.
    c) say, "You don't have to believe me but it's true."

Then Matt comes over and says, "What's the big deal? I've
stayed up all night." So you say . . .
    a) "Look who's here—Big Mouth."
    b) "Mind your own beeswax."
    c) "Really. That's interesting."

Katie says, "Isn't Matt your cousin?" And you say . . .
    a) "Don't remind me."
    b) "I'm his cousin but he's not mine."
    c) "Yes."

1. Which child is misbehaving in the sandbox?

2. True or False
   You should start down a slide when another kid is still on the
      slide.
   The best place in the playground to sit and read is at the
      bottom of the slide.
   This is the proper way to climb the slide.

Four
Playground
Bonus
Questions

3. When you are at the top of the jungle gym, which of these things would Aunt Delia most like to hear you yell?
"I can hang from two hands."
"I can hang from one hand."
"I can hang from no hands."

4. Uncle Jerry climbs to the top of the jungle gym to join you. In which of these conversations are you the most welcoming?
Uncle Jerry: "Hi. Can I sit up here, too?"
You: "No."
Uncle Jerry: "But it's a free country."
You: "Not for uncles."

Uncle Jerry: "Hi. Can I sit up here, too?"
You: "Be my guest."

BUS MANNERS

You and your Uncle Jerry are waiting
for the bus. There are several people
waiting with you. The bus pulls up.

Do you butt in front of everyone shouting, "Me first, me
first, me first"?

Do you fall into line without pushing or shoving?

Do you refuse to get on and demand a taxi instead?

4 MANNERS EXPRESS

**Bus & Nose
Bonus Question**

As soon as you get on and sit down, you
notice that the man sitting next to you
has a booger hanging out of his nose.

Do you poke Uncle Jerry, point at the
booger and giggle?

Do you say to the man, "Excuse me,
sir, but a booger is hanging out of
your nose"?

Do you look out the window and
pretend you didn't notice?

Three stops later all the seats are taken, and two old ladies, who take five minutes just to climb on the bus because they can barely walk, stand in front of you and your uncle. Your uncle gets right up and offers one of them his seat.

Do you get up and say to the other old lady, "Would you like my seat"?

Do you look down and pretend you don't see her?

Your stop is next. How do you get the driver to stop?
>Shout, "Stop the bus, I'm going to be sick."
>Let Uncle Jerry ring the bell.
>Sing, "We're here because we're here because we're here because we're here. We're here because we're here because we're here because we're here."

The bus pulls up to the curb. How do you get off?
>Charge to the door, shouting, "Outta my way or I'll throw up on you."
>Say, "Excuse me, please," as you walk to the door so that people can make room for you to get through.
>Announce, "Attention all riders. The king of the bus is getting off here. As I approach the door, everyone must bow and hand over five dollars."

Facial Expression Chart

Which expression is the
most likely to get you
what you want?

Which is the least likely?

You are playing and Aunt Delia wants a turn. In which of these conversations are you behaving generously and kindly?

Aunt Delia: "May I please have a turn?"
You: "No."

Aunt Delia: "May I please have a turn?"
You: "Yes."
Aunt Delia: "Thank you."
You: "Ha, ha, I was just kidding. You can have a turn after I finish this game."
Five minutes later. The game is over.
Aunt Delia: "Okay, it's my turn now?"
You: "What are you talking about?"
Aunt Delia: "You said when you finished, I could have a turn."
You: "I did not!"

Aunt Delia: "May I please have a turn?"
You: "Beg."
Aunt Delia: "I will not. That's insulting."
You: "Just say, 'Pretty please.' "
Aunt Delia: "No."
You: "Come on, Auntie Delia. Just say those two little words and you get a turn."
Aunt Delia: "No."
You: "Okay. But you're just hurting yourself."

Aunt Delia: "May I please have a turn?"
You don't say anything.
Aunt Delia: "I said, 'May I please have a turn?' "
You still don't say anything.
Aunt Delia: "MAY I PLEASE HAVE A TURN?!!!"
You: "You don't have to shout, Aunt Delia. That's so rude. I was going to let you play, but now that you've yelled at me, you don't deserve it."

LOSING MANNERS

Your cousin Matt just beat you at
Monopoly. He owned Boardwalk with two
hotels and you landed on it. Too bad. What do you do?
Throw all the money you owe him in his face.
Throw his hotels in his face.
Throw the Monopoly board in his face.
Scream, "Cheater, liar, jerk."
Say, "I guess you won, Matt. Good game."

SHOPPING MANNERS

You and your aunt are entering the store just as some other
shoppers are coming out.

> Do you shake their hands and say, "I hope you'll vote for
> me in November"?
>
> Do you hold the door for them?
>
> Do you trip them?

"What do you want to buy first, Aunt Delia?" "Perfume," she says. You follow her over to the perfume display. What do you do while she talks to the saleslady?

Wait patiently.

Spray perfume on yourself and, as people walk by, say, "Smell me."

The saleslady sprays some perfume on your aunt's wrist. Your aunt invites you to sniff it. What do you say if you like it?

"Will you marry me?"

"That's a big improvement on your regular smell, Aunt Delia."

"Oh-la-la! I like that."

Now your aunt wants to buy some underwear but she doesn't know where the underwear department is. While she stands in line to pay for the perfume, you decide to help her. You go over to the Information Booth. What do you say?

"Hey, man, which way to the undies?"

"My aunt wants to buy a brassiere size one hundred, underpants size two. Where should she go?"

"Would you please tell me where ladies' underwear is?"

The man informs you that ladies' underwear is sold on the second floor. You and your aunt have to walk through the store to the escalator. She asks you to hold her hand so you don't get lost.

Do you say, "Catch me first," and run away?

Do you say, "I'm too old"?

Do you hold her hand even though you're embarrassed?

Who is riding the escalator properly?

Which of these things should you be sure to do while riding the escalator?

Pinch people's behinds.

Hold on to the rail.

Now you are in the underwear department and Aunt Delia says to wait right there while she tries on some things.

Do you obey?

Do you stretch out on the floor so shoppers have to step over you and moan, "I'm so bored. When are you going to buy *me* something?"

Do you peek in all the dressing rooms?

Your aunt does not find any underwear that she likes but she thanks you for being so patient. "Now it's your turn," she says. "Let's go to the kids' department." When you arrive, what do you say to the saleslady?

"Guess what? I just saw ten naked ladies."

"I'm size eight. Bring out everything you've got and make it snappy."

"Could I please see some T-shirts and shorts, size eight?"

You select a few T-shirts and shorts to try on. Your aunt starts to come into the dressing room to help you change, but you'd rather change in private.

Do you put a sign on the door, "Keep out all aunts"?

Do you let Aunt Delia in but make her face the wall while you change?

Do you say, "I'd rather try these on by myself"?

Unfortunately, nothing you try on looks good. What do you say to the saleslady?

"All these are ugly."

"I don't think any of these is quite right. Do you have anything else?"

Now the saleslady brings you a few more things.

> Do you say, "Thank you"?
>
> Do you say, "What's your take-home pay?"
>
> Do you say, "Give me your phone number. I'd like to call you for a date"?

The saleslady peeks her head in the dressing room while you are changing and says, "How ya doing?"

> Do you scream?
>
> Do you say, "I suppose that you just heard me tell my aunt that I don't want *her* in here, so why in the world would I want *you* when we're not even related"?
>
> Do you say, "Excuse me, but I'd like to try these on in private"?

Oh, dear. The shirt you want costs twenty dollars. It might be too much for your aunt to spend.

> Do you say, "Aunt Delia, are you too poor to buy this?"
>
> Do you say, "It costs twenty dollars, Aunt Delia, is that too much? If it is, I'll find something else"?
>
> Do you say, "If you really loved me, Aunt Delia, you'd buy this for me"?

On the way out of the store, your aunt discovers that the down escalator is broken. You have to take the elevator. The elevator doors open.

> Do you wait until everyone gets out before getting on?
>
> Do you announce, "This is the president of the United States with his Aunt Delia. As soon as I get inside this elevator, all passengers will please recite, 'The Pledge of Allegiance' "?
>
> Do you dash in yelling, "I want to push the buttons, I want to push the buttons"?

While you ride down in the elevator, what do you do?

>Keep quiet.

>Say, "Guess what, everyone. My aunt has a dead rat in her garage."

>Put on your new T-shirt and ask everyone how they like it.

>Blow your nose on your sleeve.

GIVING COMPLIMENTS

You and your friend Adam
are in the finals of the spelling bee.
He wins after you make a mistake spelling
manners with only one *N*. What do you say to him?

"I'm really a much better speller
than you. You just got lucky."

"The judges cheated."

"All your words were easier."

"I wanted to lose."

"Congratulations."

Uncle Jerry invites you to come out and see his garden. He shows you his fifteen rosebushes all gorgeous with flowers. "I planted these, I nursed them, I pruned them," says Uncle Jerry proudly. What do you say?

"Big deal."

"Can I go ride my bike now?"

"They look beautiful, Uncle Jerry. You did a great job."

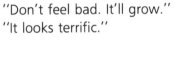

Your friend Mindy is very excited. She just had a haircut and wants to show it to you. When she arrives, you are horrified. Her hair is much too short, especially her bangs. "How do you like my hair?" she asks. What do you say?

"What hair?"

"It's almost right but not quite. If you give me those scissors, I'll fix it."

"Don't feel bad. It'll grow."

"It looks terrific."

You asked your Aunt Delia to buy you a Walkman but she said you would have to wait until your birthday to get one. Then you go over to Julie's and she shows you what her mom just bought her—a Walkman. What do you say?

"Oh, Julie, lucky you."

"That's not the good kind. The good kind plays tapes *and* AM and FM."

"You think you're so great just 'cause you have a Walkman."

"If you were my friend, you'd give it to me."

"I've got something else new, too," says Julie. And she takes off her jacket and shows you her cow sweatshirt. What do you say to her?

"Moo."

"Blue's not your color."

"Sweatshirts make you sweat, and sweat makes you smell."

"It's really better if your mom or aunt doesn't get you everything you want."

"Oh, I love that sweatshirt. It looks so cute on you."

"It's not fair. First you get the Walkman, now the sweatshirt. I hate you."

Tricky Question 4

Who is using the soupspoon properly?

HOLIDAY MANNERS

It's time to get ready to go to Thanksgiving dinner. Your aunt and uncle will be there, your grandma and grandpa, your cousins Michelle, Simon, and Matt. What should you wear?

Nothing.

A tutu.

A clean shirt and pants.

Your mom says that you have to brush your hair.

Do you say, "I already did it once this week"?

Do you brush and comb it neatly?

Do you say, "I like it messy. That's the way I want it"?

After a long ride in the car, you finally arrive. Everyone is so excited to see you.

Do you give Aunt Delia, Uncle Jerry, Grandma, and Grandpa a big hug and a kiss?

Do you scream, "No kisses, I hate kisses"?

Do you hug Aunt Delia and Grandma but hold your nose so you don't have to smell them?

Your grandma says, "My goodness, look how you've grown."
    Do you say, "And you've shrunk"?
    Do you say, "Thanks"?
    Do you say, "Don't blame me. It's not my fault"?

Your mom reminds you to say hello to the baby, your cousin
Simon, whom you've never met because he was just born.

Do you admire him and let him hold
    your finger in his fist?
Do you say, "Hi, Baldie, where's your
    hair"?
Do you say, "Hey, dude," and pass
    him a football?
Do you say, "Aunt Delia, don't hold
    him, hold me!"?

Your cousin Michelle comes downstairs to
say hello. She's twelve. What do you say
to her?
    "Hi, Michelle, your slip is showing."
    "Hi, Michelle, it's nice to see you."
    "Hi, Michelle, bye, Michelle."

Everyone sits down and Aunt Delia carries the turkey to the table.
    Do you say, "Aunt Delia, that turkey looks delicious"?
    Do you say, "Aunt Delia, that turkey looks like Uncle Jerry"?
    Do you say, "What's the story, Auntie? Did you cook the
        cat?"

Aunt Delia asks if you want everything: turkey, cranberry sauce, creamed onions, string beans, and stuffing.

> Do you say, "Nix on the stuffing, stuff the string beans in the garbage, and string the onions up a tree"?
>
> Do you say, "Are creamed onions those little white balls floating in glue? If so, no"?
>
> Do you say, "I'll have white meat turkey, cranberry sauce, and two string beans, please"?

Your aunt gives you your plate. On it she put one creamed onion and it is touching the turkey meat.

> Do you ignore it?
>
> Do you refuse to eat the turkey because the onion touched it?
>
> Do you cry?

You eat some cranberry sauce and suddenly realize that it's homemade with little bits of orange rind on top. Oh, no!

> Do you say, "Excuse me, Aunt Delia, but I think there are bird droppings on the cranberry sauce"?
>
> Do you say, "I hate this kind of cranberry sauce. I like Ocean Spray in a can"?
>
> Do you leave it on your plate and say nothing?
>
> Do you pass your plate back and say, "Kindly get this ugly red stuff off my plate"?

Which of these are appropriate subjects for Thanksgiving dinner conversation?

Whether the turkey knew it was going to die.

The time cousin Michelle laughed so hard while eating that a hot dog came out of her nose.

Stinkbombs.

Pilgrims.

If you wanted to make Aunt Delia really happy, which of these would you do?

Tell her you love the food.

Shout, "Food fight," and throw turkey at your cousins.

Stir the gravy with your finger.

You are finished eating before your Uncle Jerry is finished carving.

Do you sit patiently and wait until everyone else has finished eating?

Do you disappear under the table and steal napkins from everyone's lap?

Do you put your head on your plate and go to sleep?

It's time to go home. What's the best way to show everyone how much you love them?

> Give them each a big hug and a kiss and thank Aunt Delia for the delicious dinner.
>
> Say, ''Some Thanksgiving. The only thing I liked was the white meat turkey.''
>
> Say, ''So long Aunt Delia, Uncle Jerry, Grandma, Grandpa, Matt, Michelle, and Baldie. See you at Christmas. Bring big presents.''